First published in 2011
by Hodder Children's Books.
This paperback edition published in 2011

Copyright © Mick Inkpen 2011

Hodder Children's Books
338 Euston Road, London NW1 3BH

Hodder Children's Books Australia
Level 17/207 Kent Street, Sydney, NSW 2000

The right of Mick Inkpen to be identified as the author
and illustrator of this Work has been asserted by him in
accordance with the Copyright, Designs and Patents Act 1988.

A catalogue record of this book is
available from the British Library.

ISBN: 978 0 750 05626 7
10 9 8 7 6 5 4 3 2 1

Printed in China

Hodder Children's Books is a
division of Hachette Children's Books,
an Hachette UK Company
www.hachette.co.uk

Wibbly Pig has

10 balloons

But he likes
the teddy bear
balloon best.

Hodder
Children's
Books

A division of Hachette Children's Books

10

'Ten balloons!'
says Wibbly Pig.
'And all of them are mine!'
'Can I have one?'
says Tiny Pig.
So ten turns into. . .

Not the teddy bear balloon. It's my favourite.

9

'Nine balloons?'
says Scruffy Pig.
'And Tiny Pig's got one!
Nine balloons and one
make ten.
And that leaves me
with none!'

Alright, Scruffy Pig. You can have one too. But not the teddy bear balloon.

8

'Eight balloons!'
says Spotty Pig.
'And Scruffy's got one too!'
'Alright, choose one,'
sighs Wibbly Pig.
The one he picks is. . .

. . . blue.

**7**

Wibbly Pig has
seven balloons.
But not for very long.
He's only just stopped
counting them. . .

Ding Dong!

. . .when Pig Ears
comes along.

And not just Pig Ears,
Big Pig too.
And Pig Twins,
both of them.
And someone else
he's never met,
Big Pig's sister's friend!

Thank you
very much
Wibbly.

6 5 4 3

So now he has to
count again.
Not **six,**
not **five,**
not **four.**
Just **three** balloons
is all he has. . .

Ding Dong!
Ding Dong!
Ding Dong!

But who's **this** at the door!

Big Pig's sister
wants one too.
'Let me have one.
Let me!'
She pouts and shouts
and stamps about.
But Wibbly
won't agree.

She flounces out.
She flounces in.
(She knows she'll get her way.)

She holds her breath,
and stares. . .
and glares. . .

till Wibbly says. . .

'OK.'

She **grabs** the
strings from Wibbly.
'The pink one,
with the bow!
That's the one I want!'
she squeals.
And lets the
others go!

She lets the others go!

No balloons for
Wibbly Pig.
He wants to cry.
No balloons for
Wibbly Pig,

but then, nearby. . .

. . .a little voice,
a weeny voice,
(a Tiny voice)
is squealing,
'Please get me down!
Please get me down!
I'm up here. . .

. . .on the ceiling!'

'This balloon is much too big!
You can have it, Wibbly Pig!'

Wibbly sniffs. . .
helps Tiny down. . .
then sniffs some more. . .
and stops.
'Thank you Tiny Pig,'
he says.

And that. . .

is when. . .

Wibbly Pig and Tiny Pig
    sit sadly in the park.
They talk away the afternoon.
    They talk until it's dark.

'No balloons,' sighs Wibbly Pig.
    'And I started out with ten!
That teddy bear balloon was best.
    I had three left, and then. . .'

But Tiny Pig's not listening.
    He's staring at the moon.
There's something
    floating past it. . .

. . .the teddy bear balloon!

'My teddy bear
balloon came back!'
says Wibbly,
with a grin. . .

And Tiny's grinning too
because. . .

. . .one came back for him!

This igloo book belongs to:

....

igloobooks

Published in 2014
by Igloo Books Ltd
Cottage Farm
Sywell
NN6 0BJ
www.igloobooks.com

LEO002 0514
2 4 6 8 10 9 7 5 3 1
ISBN 978-1-78440-082-8

Illustrated by Jo De Ruiter

Printed and manufactured in China

Little Ted's BIG ADVENTURE

JO DE RUITER

igloobooks

One morning,
Little Ted woke
up and saw the
sky was grey.

"I know just
what to do," he
said, "I'll go on
holiday."

Ted hurried off to clean his teeth and wash his sleepy face.

He grabbed his little squeaky duck and quickly packed his case.

Ted hopped onto a speedy jet that zoomed him off to Spain.

"I do prefer the beach," he said, "instead of all that rain."

He built a huge sandcastle, made of seaweed, shells and sand.

Then sang and danced all evening, with a cool flamenco band.

In France, Ted bought the biggest, yummy treat he'd ever seen,

Made with chocolate sauce and caramel and sticky, mint ice cream!

He climbed the
Eiffel Tower all
the way without a stop.
Ted felt worn out when
halfway up, but made
it to the top.

In Italy, Ted ate some slippy pasta with his bread.

The pasta slithered through his fork and splattered Little Ted!

Ted hired a floating gondola
which carried him away.

He floated down the Venice streets,
while singing all the way.

In Egypt, Little Ted explored a dark and creepy tomb.

He saw a spooky mummy standing in the murky gloom!

"A scary thing!" cried Little Ted.

He quickly dashed outside and tumbled down the pyramid just like a bumpy slide!

In China, Ted walked on the Wall and leapt right off the side!

He landed on a panda bear who took him for a ride.

Then, afterward, he joined
the panda for a bite or two.
They lazed on bright, green jungle
leaves while munching on bamboo.

"I think Great Britain will
be next," decided Little Ted.
So, off he went to meet the queen
for tea with jam and bread.

That afternoon, Ted went to watch a football match for fun.

"Come on, you reds!" sang Little Ted. "Now, score another one!"

Ted travelled to Australia
and met a wallaby,
Who tucked Ted in its
little pouch and let
him ride for free.

They leapt over a crocodile
who opened up one eye.

Its jaws went SNAP!
"Look out!" cried Ted,
as they went
bouncing by.

America was next. Ted said, "I've heard it's pretty good. I want to visit all the famous stars in Hollywood."

He boogied at a disco and he met a movie star,

Who whizzed him round
a racetrack in his flashy
racing car.

By now, poor Ted was feeling tired. "I'm quite worn out," he said. "I've loved my little holiday, but now I need my bed!"

"It's been a great adventure and I must come back one day." Ted packed his case and wearily he headed on his way.

At last, Ted reached his little
house and snuggled into bed.

"I've had a lot of fun, but now
I'm glad I'm home," he said.